The Corked Incident

Dr. Jesse V. McClain IV DNP, APRN, FWS

DEDICATION

For Kelsey, my love and partner in every adventure—your
unwavering support fills my world with warmth.
For Noel and Winter, my greatest inspirations—may your
curiosity and imagination always lead you to thrilling
discoveries.

ACKNOWLEDGMENTS

First and foremost, to my wife, Kelsey—your love, encouragement, and belief in me made this book possible. Your support fuels my creativity, and I am endlessly grateful for you.

To my daughters, Noel and Winter—your boundless curiosity and joy remind me why storytelling matters. May you always chase adventure and embrace mystery.

To my friends and family who listened to my endless ramblings about this story—your patience and insights helped shape it into what it is today.

To my six Advanced Practice Provider colleagues and friends —thank you for stepping into this world. I hope it intrigues, surprises, and entertains you as much as it did me while writing it.

TABLE OF CONTENTS

Acknowledgments

Prologue

PROLOGUE

Jamie leaned against the desk in the cramped office, arms crossed as he watched the others sift through stacks of folders and papers from physical therapy facilities that required signing. The whiteboard in the corner was cluttered with hastily erased notes from morning rounds, a testament to the relentless pace of the neurology service they all managed. However, also written on that whiteboard was the phrase; *In Case of Emergency, don't call us, call 911.*

It was the end of another demanding week, but instead of heading home, the team was packing up for their annual scheduling discussion—this year, in an entirely new setting.

"I still think we could've done this at your place," Abby muttered, flipping through a printout.

"We've outgrown that," Traci countered, shoving a stack of documents into her bag. "Besides, I think we could all use a change of scenery."

"100%" Eve exclaimed.

Jamie sighed. "You just don't want to sit in my kitchen again, fighting over who gets the last cup of coffee."

Lori chuckled from across the room. "Don't act like you and Kayla don't love hosting, Wine Doc. Kayla always has the best cookies—and you have the best wine."

"This isn't about wine Lori," Jamie mockingly replied, rolling his eyes but unable to suppress a small smile. The nickname had stuck long ago, a playful jab at Jamie's hobby that had somehow become part of his identity in the group.

Abby glanced at the clock. "If we don't get moving, we're going to hit traffic. Lake house or not, I'm not spending my Friday night in gridlock."

It was Sara's idea to take the scheduling meeting offsite this year. What had once been a casual evening at Jamie and Kayla's house had grown into an increasingly stressful ordeal, as the neurology service became busier, more demanding and grown in numbers with the addition of Lori. The lake house promised quiet, focus, and—hopefully—solutions to the growing challenges of balancing their call schedule.

"Alright, alright," Jamie said, grabbing his locked duffle bag and laptop. "Let's hit the road. And for the record, I'm still skeptical about this place. Two hours away too? Damn!"

"You're only skeptical because it's near a lake," Nina teased, slinging her coat over one shoulder. "You can't pretend you're not going to enjoy this weekend."

The group laughed as they shuffled out of the office, their banter masking the undercurrent of tension that came with their work. Being advanced practice providers in neurology wasn't just a job—it was a constant balancing act of critical cases, long hours, and the ever-present weight of responsibility. The retreat was a chance to step back, have some fun and rework the on-call schedule for the following year, but it was also a reminder of how much they relied on each other to keep things running smoothly.

As they headed for the door, Jamie hesitated, glancing back at the whiteboard. The mess of scribbles and numbers felt symbolic of their lives—always in motion, always a little chaotic. With a deep breath, he turned and followed the others, the quiet hope in his chest that this weekend might finally bring some relaxation.

BOTTLE 1

THE ANNUAL RETREAT

The scent of pine and the crisp lake breeze filled the air as Lori stepped out of the car, her gaze sweeping over the secluded lake house nestled among the trees. It had been a year since the group of seven Advanced Practice Providers last gathered for their annual retreat. This year's agenda was the same: work out their neurology on-call schedule, drink too much wine, and enjoy a weekend away from the stress of their hospital jobs.

Traci was the first to arrive, followed by Jamie and then Nina.

"First to arrive, first to pick bedroom." Traci stated

"Have at it girl." Nina said, "I am right behind you."

Jamie picked third and as he entered his room, Traci greeted him like a cat springing from the bushes, "You know, I don't appreciate how you switched our dictation microphones last week."

"What are you talking about?" Jamie questioned.

"They told me you switched them out because yours was not working appropriately. Next time, just ask." Traci angrily stated.

"Sure, no problem." Jamie agreed quickly just to get her to go away so he could unpack but now, so startled by the confrontation, he just threw his duffel bag down, grabbed his waiter's key and headed back downstairs.

Jamie, ever the life of the party, returned to his car after dropping the key off in the kitchen to unload his prized wine crate. "Ladies and gentlemen," he declared with a flourish, "The Wine Doctor for the weekend has arrived! Prepare your palates for an unparalleled journey."

Eve rolled her eyes with a smile. "We get it, Wine Doc. You're fancy."

Traci chuckled as she grabbed a bag of groceries. "Just don't try to impress us with anything that requires more than two syllables. We're here to relax, not study."

As the group trickled inside, laughter and banter filled the spacious living room. Abby and Nina were already inspecting the kitchen, and Sara was flipping through channels on the oversized TV. They all needed this weekend. The grind of back-to-back shifts and the pressure of saving lives were taxing, even for seasoned professionals like the seven of them.

Lori, the newest to the group, dropped her bag by the door and stretched. "This place is perfect. Who found it again?"

"That would be me," Sara said sarcastically. "You're welcome."

"Well, Sara," Nina said, peeking through the large glass doors leading to the deck, "I'll admit, you nailed it. Look at that view! This is much better than just meeting at Kayla and Jamie's house."

Outside, the lake shimmered under the afternoon sun, framed by a backdrop of tall pines. The deck, complete with a fire pit and lounge chairs, promised long, lazy evenings.

Jamie walked in carrying a bottle of champagne, holding it aloft like a trophy. "Alright, enough soberness, Let's christen this retreat properly. Who's ready for the first pop?"

Abby smirked, leaning against the counter. "You sure you don't want to save that for later? It's not even five yet."

"It's a retreat, Abby. Time to 'wine' down," Jamie shot back, expertly peeling away the foil.

The group gathered around the kitchen island as Jamie angled the bottle. "Now, observe," he said, his voice adopting a faux-teacher tone. "The key to opening champagne is finesse. You don't want it to explode—it should sound like the whisper of a princess and not the fart of a whore."

"Just open it, Jamie," Eve teased. "You say that every time."

Jamie smiled but continued his mock demonstration, his fingers firmly gripping the cork. "Patience, my dear Eve. As I always say, nothing kills you faster than rushing— well, except for an on-call week of course."

Everyone turned and annoyingly walked away into adjacent rooms. Jamie removed the cage and then worked on the bottle and cork.

"Where is everyone going" Jamie questioned.

They waved him off and while he remained in the kitchen, the others scattered into various nearby rooms. Jamie sat the bottle on the counter, cage, cork and all while attempting to persuade his friends to return. "Come on guys, I am just joking around" Jamie explained. He returned to the kitchen after acquiring zero takers for his demonstration.

"Well, I guess I will continue to unpack." Jamie disappointingly stated. The bottle left on the island. Jamie reached into a box and began to unpack a few more bottles of wine placing each one on the rack in the kitchen. He then opened the refrigerator, when suddenly, he was jolted on the side of his head. Seeing stars, he yelled out for help. The group, startled by the sudden holler, turned back and ran into the kitchen.

By the time most of them returned to the kitchen, Jamie was seen staggering and then he fell onto the island. Traci, already present, dropped the bottle shattering it on the tiled floor. Jamie clutched his head, a stunned look on his face, before collapsing onto the rug.

"Jamie?" Lori's laughter evaporated as she crouched beside him.

"Come on, Jamie, stop messing around," Traci said, though her voice wavered.

Abby, the most neurology experienced among them (second to Jamie), knelt next to Lori, feeling for a pulse. "It wasn't an accident" he whispered as he stopped breathing.

Abby "I cannot find a pulse"

The room erupted into chaos. Nina scrambled to grab the first aid kit from her luggage. Lori began chest compressions while Abby barked instructions.

"What the hell just happened?" Eve asked, her voice rising in panic.

"We need to get him stabilized. Can someone call 911?" Abby anxiously stated.

"Shoddy signal" Eve reminded the group.

"I swear I did not do this" Traci stated, disbelief etched on her face. "How could—"

"Quiet!" Abby snapped, her focus unshaken. "We need to focus."

As Lori continued compressions, Nina returned with the kit. "What should we do now? The hospital is hours away!"

Abby grabbed a bag valve mask from Nina's kit and positioned it over Jamie's mouth. "We stabilize him first. Then we figure out the rest."

"Wait, there is glass everywhere" Sara said, her eyes scanning the floor."

The group froze, their eyes darting to the shattered glass on the floor.

"What the hell is going on?" Eve whispered.

The tension in the room thickened as Abby continued to pump air into Jamie's lungs.

"Keep going, Lori," Abby said, her voice calm but firm. She shifted her position to check Jamie's pupils with the small flashlight from the kit. "Damn it, his pupil is blown. He must have some sort of bleed. He is herniating."

"This doesn't make sense," Nina said, pacing the room. "What happened?"

"I have no idea" Traci replied, though she sounded uncertain.

"You have no idea?" Sara interrupted. "You were in here with him!"

"I was not! I got in here just before all of you." Traci defensively stated. "I grabbed the bottle on my way in! Hell, you, Sara, didn't even come in until after they started CPR."

"Shut it" Eve suggested, though her voice quivered.

Lori grunted with effort as she continued chest compressions. "Can we stop arguing? Jamie's dying over here!"

Nina stopped pacing, her hands on her hips. "And what are we supposed to do, Lori? We're in the middle of nowhere with no signal and no hospital for miles. If we don't figure this out—"

"Enough!" Abby snapped, her voice cutting through the panic. "We'll debate physics later. Lori, switch with me. I'll do compressions."

Lori leaned back, her arms trembling from exhaustion, and Abby immediately took over. "Eve, grab your cell phone; Nina, check the landline to see if it's working since our cell phones keep cutting in and out. Traci, look for anything that could help—ice packs, towels, anything."

The room buzzed frantically with energy as everyone scrambled to follow Abby's instructions. Nina darted toward the phone on the wall, lifting the receiver to her ear. Her face fell.

"It's dead. No dial tone."

"Of course it is," Sara muttered. "Classic horror movie setup. No cell signal and now no dial tone."

"This isn't a joke!" Nina snapped, slamming the receiver back into place.

"Who is laughing Nina?" Sara shot back.

Meanwhile, Traci returned with a bag of frozen peas and a dish towel. "This is all I could find in the freezer."

Abby gestured for her to apply it to Jamie's temple. "Better than nothing. Keep the swelling down while we try to stabilize him."

"Should we drive him to the hospital?" Lori asked, her voice tinged with desperation.

"And risk moving him with a suspected brain bleed?" Abby shook her head. "Not unless it's our only option."

As they worked, Eve crouched near the broken glass, her eyes narrowing. "This... this isn't right. Look at the label. It certainly does not appear normal at all. It appears altered and certainly not made from any winery. It sure appears as if somebody must've swapped it."

"Swapped it?" Traci echoed. "When? We've all been here together the whole time."

"Sure, but we all were in different rooms. That is, unless someone planted it," Eve said, her voice barely above a whisper. "And? Girl, you were holding it when we arrived!"

"What the hell are you saying?" Nina demanded, crossing her arms.

"Yeah!" Traci reiterated Nina's thought.

Eve stood with a grim expression. "I'm saying someone could've tampered with the bottle. Maybe it wasn't an accident; like Jamie said."

The room fell silent, except for the rhythm of Abby's compressions. The possibility hung in the air, heavy and suffocating.

"That's insane," Sara said, though she looked more unnerved than convinced. "Why would anyone, let alone, any of us want to hurt Jamie? That doesn't make sense."

"Does any of this make sense?" Eve shot back. "Where were you when this all went down?"

"Oh, stop it. Now, is not the time Eve." Sara said.

"If he doesn't wake up soon, we'll have no choice but to risk the drive. Wait, I have a dial tone. I am calling 9-1-1." Nina mentioned.

Lori broke the silence. "If this wasn't an accident..., are we saying it's one of us who did this to Jamie?"

Nina shouted "they will be here in 45-60 minutes"

Lori's words hit like a thunderclap. No one spoke, their eyes darting around the room, scanning each other's faces for signs of guilt or betrayal.

"Stop," Abby said firmly. "We're not jumping to conclusions. Right now, our priority is Jamie. 60 minutes Nina? Are you serious"

"That's what they said. They told me that we are literally in the middle of nowhere" explained Nina.

But as the group huddled together, trying to make sense of the chaos, one thought refused to leave anyone's mind: If this wasn't an accident, who could they trust?

The revelation of mismatched label raised suspicions that Jamie's accident might have been orchestrated, leaving the group to grapple with the chilling possibility of foul play.

BOTTLE 2

AN UNLIKELY ACCIDENT

The sun dipped below the horizon, its golden light reflecting off the lake in shimmering ripples. Inside the cabin, the mood was anything but serene. Abby, still kneeling beside Jamie, checked his vitals for what felt like the hundredth time. Jamie, who was subsequently moved to the living room for what Nina believed to be more comfortable for him, lay motionless and pulseless.

Lori, still compressing the bag valve mask every so often, nervously asked, "He should have a pulse by now, right? This... this isn't normal."

Abby exhaled sharply; her hands steady but her voice betrayed her frustration. "We are doing everything we can. EMS is on the way."

"Should we just give up at this point?" Sara asked

"Oh, you'd love that miss I wasn't even there when this happened." Lori sarcastically exclaimed.

"Oh, shut up Lori, I am just as upset as you." Sara shot back.

Traci sat cross-legged on the floor, her back against the wall. "Should we be doing more?"

"And what do you suggest we do?" Abby snapped. "We're hours away from the nearest ER and EMS said that we were in the middle of nowhere"—her glare briefly shifted to Eve, who rolled her eyes— "and even if we got him there, there's no guarantee they'd do anything we are not already doing other than intubate him."

"We could do a cric" Nina casually mentioned.

"Good grief Nina" Abby said with her mouth wide open as if she never heard such an egregious recommendation.

"Damn it!" Sara chimed in; her arms crossed as she leaned against the kitchen doorway. "We still do not even know what happened."

Eve's voice was sharp, her pace quickening. "What if there's more going on here? Traci, you were there when we arrived; and you were holding the bottle!"

"I swear I did not do this." Traci exclaimed "Why don't you pester Sara to ask her whereabouts instead of me?

Plus, she wants to off him now anyway."

"Oh, shut up Traci" Sara angrily shot back.

"Here we go," Nina muttered, rubbing her temples. "Eve's diving headfirst into one of her conspiracy theories again."

"It's not a conspiracy theory, girl!" Eve shot back. Her eyes blazing. "Something's not right about this. Bottles don't just get switched and people don't get knocked unconscious that easily. Jamie's got the reflexes of a damn cat. How did this happen? That is, unless he had his back turned to whomever whacked him."

"Eve!?! Maybe it's just stress," Sara offered flatly, her tone practical. "Fatigue? Too much wine, maybe?"

"And you seriously think that is all it is? Jamie died because of stress?" Eve retorted.

"Jamie is not dead!!!" Abby cried out "He seems to have a faint pulse. But keep bagging"

"Come on, Sara. You're the one who's always talking about looking deeper. Aren't you even a little curious about how strange this is? And furthermore, Jamie had not even started drinking and did not fall until we got there. Well, until most of us came into the kitchen I guess."

"Come on Eve, stop it" Sara pleaded.

"What if he just bumped his head?" Lori asked.

"Enough!" Abby's voice cut through the escalating argument like a scalpel. "This isn't helping Jamie one bit. And unless someone has actual proof that something shady happened, we are treating this as an accident. Period. Plus, the police are coming with EMS, I am sure. If we start accusing one another, so will the police and we do not need that at all. This was just an accident! Got it?"

For a moment the room fell silent, except for the hum of the ceiling fan overhead.

Then a faint groan broke the tension.

"Jamie?" Lori rushed to his side as his eyelids fluttered weakly.

Jamie let out a low, pained sound, he was gone.

Abby leaned in, "Shit! He's gone."

Abby nodded, refocusing her attention on Jamie's vitals, or lack thereof.

Sara stepped into the kitchen, her steps slow and deliberate. But as she approached the counter, she froze.

"Uh... guys?" Her voice was tense, sharp enough to draw everyone's attention.

Abby sighed, exasperated. "What now, Sara?"

"Someone's been in here." Sara mentioned.

The group crowded into the kitchen; confusion etched across their faces. Sara pointed to the refrigerator door, which hung slightly ajar. A faint trail of condensation streaked from the fridge to the counter.

"Did anyone leave this open?" Sara asked, her voice tight.

"No," Traci said, glancing around. "We've all been in the living room since... you know."

Eve crouched near the adjacent corner of the kitchen, her sharp eyes catching a glint of something small and round. She reached out, her fingers brushing against it before lifting it into the light.

"What is that?" Nina asked, leaning closer.

"It's the cork," Eve said, her voice low.

"I wondered where that went!" Traci reflexively responded.

The group fell silent as they stared at the object in her hand. The glass-free cork looked splintered, its edges jagged, embossed with wording which were written in French. Faint traces of a sticky, amber-like residue clung to its surface.

"Is that... glue?" Lori asked, her voice trembling.

Eve turned the cork over in her fingers, her expression darkening. "I don't know if it's glue or molasses, but it is definitely sticky."

Abby, who had now finally left Jamie's side, grabbed the cork from Eve, inspecting it with a clinical eye. Her jaw tightened. "This doesn't make sense."

"It makes perfect sense," Eve said, her voice hard. "As I have been stating, someone switched the bottle! Which, if it was not one of us proves that someone else had to be in this house."

"How are you so sure that someone switched the bottles?" Nina asked, "It is literally just a cork."

"Look! these words" as Eve pointed on the cork, "these words on the cork are in French." Eve continued "The label on the bottle did not look French. This cork says, La Cuvée blah blah blah and Jamie previously taught us that the cork and label matching is how wineries prevented fraud."

"Really?" Traci asked "Fraud?"

"Yes" Eve answered. "This is why a waiter will present the cork to you at a table in a restaurant. It is not for you to smell and look all fancy, but rather for you to look at the cork and the label to ensure the name on the cork matches the name on the label. The label and the cork must always match. This cork and that label do not match!" As she gestured to the table where the label currently rested.

The realization sent a ripple of unease through the group. The air seemed to grow heavier, the shadows longer.

The tampered bottle revealed that Jamie's death was quite possibly deliberate. Suspicion fell within the group, each member now wondering: Who could have done this—and why?

BOTTLE 3

A PATTERN EMERGES

The living room was eerily quiet, the warmth of the fire doing little to dispel the chill that had settled over the group. Jamie's lifeless form lay on the floor, his chest unnaturally still. Abby knelt beside him.

"This doesn't add up," Nina muttered, pacing back and forth. She hugged herself tightly, her steps quick and anxious. "It just doesn't make sense."

Traci sat hunched on the arm of the couch, her arms

wrapped around her knees. "It's not possible," she said firmly, though her trembling voice betrayed her fear. "This doesn't happen to someone like Jamie. It's too... freakish."

"Traci," Eve said softly but firmly. "You don't know that. We all know Jamie. He always had a flare for the dramatic. He might've done something careless."

Traci's head snapped up. "Are you saying this is his fault?"

"That's not what she is saying," Lori replied, her voice hardening. "She is saying that sometimes shit happens."

"Shit happens?" Sara said with a puzzled look on her face as if she could not believe Lori suggested that.

"Yeah, shit happens Sara!" Lori snapped back.

Abby stood and turned to face the group. "We can't let

our emotions get the better of us. Right now, we need to focus." She swallowed hard, unwilling to finish the thought.

Sara, leaning against the fireplace mantel, crossed her arms. "The real question is: did something—or someone—cause this?"

The room fell silent as the weight of her words sunk in.

"I've been thinking about earlier," Nina said hesitantly, breaking the quiet. "Jamie wasn't himself tonight. He seemed distracted, like he had something on his mind. He just wasn't his usual self."

"What do you mean?" Eve asked, her brow furrowing.

Nina gestured vaguely toward the table where the broken champagne bottle rested. "You know how he always made a big production about it? Talking about the vintage, the technique, all that sommelier stuff? Tonight, he just... rushed it. Like he was nervous."

Traci shifted uncomfortably, her arms tightening around herself. "I noticed that too," she said softly. "He kept checking his phone. He looked... worried."

"Worried about what?" Eve asked, her tone sharp. "Kayla and the girls were having fun at the waterpark. They are fine."

Nina snuck in under her breath, "Well, they won't be when they hear about this."

"I don't know what he was worried about," Traci admitted. "I didn't ask. I figured he'd talk about it when he was ready."

Abby walked over to Jamie's side, his phone lying beside. She hesitated, glancing at his still form. "If he was worried about something, maybe it's on here, holding up his phone."

"Wait," Traci said, standing quickly. "We can't just go through his phone and stuff. That's not right."

"Traci," Abby said, her voice calm but firm, "we need answers. If there's something on this phone that explains why Jamie was acting so strangely, we must know. For him."

"But do we really Abby?" Eve questioned.

Traci hesitated, her lips pressing into a thin line, but finally stepped aside. Abby unlocked his phone by flashing it in Jamie's lifeless face and began scrolling through the messages. Her expression darkened as she held up the screen for the others to see.

The message was from a number not listed in his

contacts.

"I know you can't wait forever. Now, share your location, so I can do what needs to be done."

The group collectively inhaled, the words carrying an ominous weight.

"What does that even mean?" Sara asked, her voice tight.

Abby scrolled further, revealing more messages from the same number:

"The cost is too great." Mysterious Number

"It's fine, just do it." Jamie

"Well, this is on you. Consider it done. I will handle everything." Mysterious Number

Eve's face went pale. "Shit; Jamie was in some kind of trouble."

"What kind of trouble?" Lori asked, her voice trembling. "We've known him for years. If he was dealing with something this big, wouldn't he have told us? Maybe at least some of us."

"Maybe he didn't think he could," Sara said. "Or maybe..." She hesitated, her voice lowering. "Maybe he thought one of us was involved."

"This is all crazy, what are you implying?" Traci asked, her tone defensive.

Sara locked eyes with her. "I'm saying we don't know what Jamie was dealing with. And until we do, we can't rule out anything—not even that someone here might have played a part."

The accusation landed like a bomb, sending shockwaves through the group.

"That's insane," Traci snapped. "We're his friends! None of us would ever hurt him."

"Then tell us what really happened while you two were in the kitchen." And though Eve made the statement, they all were thinking it. But before Traci could respond, Abby chimed in.

"Enough," Abby said sharply, cutting through the rising tension. "Pointing fingers isn't going to help us. We need to keep our heads and figure out what's going on."

Eve crossed her arms, her expression icy, "And how do you propose we do that?"

Abby glanced back at Jamie's still form, her jaw tightening. "We wait for help. They are probably not far out at this point. In the meantime, we keep looking for answers. If there's something we're missing—something Jamie was hiding—we must figure it out."

BOTTLE 4

THE TENSION BUILDS

The group was in shambles. Jamie's unidentified messages threw gasoline on the already burning fire of suspicion. While Abby and Sara stayed nearby, the others began to splinter into factions. They were in search of answers to questions they did not know.

Lori stood by the large picture window, staring out into the pitch-black forest surrounding the lake house. Her hands were clasped tightly in front of her as though praying for clarity. Traci and Nina sat at the dining table, whispering heatedly, their voices rising and falling like waves. Eve paced furiously near the fireplace, throwing sharp glances at anyone who dared to meet her gaze.

Abby rubbed her temples as she looked at Sara, who was still shaken. "What do you think those messages meant?" Abby whispered.

Sara frowned. "I don't know. It sounded like Jamie was in debt to someone and they are coming after him: Remember? 'The cost is too great. Share your location?' But in debt over what? I can't make sense of it."

"Coming after him or came after him?" Abby questioned Sara.

"But why?" Sara asked.

"Maybe his crypto? Or NFTs?" Sara questioned.

Abby sighed. "Why all this secrecy? The text messages, the way he was acting... something's not right."

Across the room, Nina threw up her hands in exasperation. "I'm telling you, it's not as complicated as you all want to make it. Jamie was stressed. He just bumped his head in the wrong place. That's all this is!"

Traci slammed her hand on the table. "Stop oversimplifying! Did you even hear the messages Abby found? He was clearly dealing with something bigger than any of us realized."

Eve stopped pacing and pointed a finger at Traci. "And how would you know? You're the one who was glued to his side all night. Maybe you know more than you're letting on."

Traci's face reddened. "Excuse me? I am sick and tired of all these implications, Eve!"

"You heard me," Eve shot back. "You were the one with him in the kitchen and the one holding the bottle when we arrived. Maybe you know what was going on, and you're just too scared to admit it."

"Yeah, and I saw you confronting him about the dictation microphone while everyone was arriving!" exclaimed Nina.

"Good grief! AHHH" Traci screamed out. "I was upset about the fact he switched my dictaphone! I never thought those would be my last words to him or I would have just let it go. So, yes, I had words with Jamie before this happened, but it certainly was not a reason to off his ass."

"Enough!" Lori's voice cut through the chaos like a scalpel. She turned from the window, her usually calm demeanor now brimming with frustration. "We're getting nowhere by tearing each other apart."

"Off his ass?" Sara shook her head and snickered under her breath.

The group fell silent, but the tension in the room was palpable.

Sara broke the quiet. "Maybe Lori's right. Let's take a step back and think logically. Jamie's acting strangely and the messages. What do we actually know?"

Abby folded her arms. "We know he was distracted and nervous all evening. We know someone was texting him about something he couldn't avoid. And we know..." Her voice wavered and she was unable to finish her statement.

Traci bit her lip. "We know he's been working crazy hours lately. What if... what if he was covering for someone? Taking on too many patients; seeing some when he is covering the hospital. Or maybe he was hiding a mistake? That could explain the stress. He wasn't back involved in all that political stuff again, was he?"

"Not that I know of." Nina answered.

"Or" Eve interjected, "what if someone was blackmailing him? That message — 'This is on you now' and 'share your location' — Well, I am not sure about y'all in Ohio, but in Florida, those are threats."

"Blackmail?" Nina asked skeptically. "Jamie was being blackmailed over what?"

Sara's eyes narrowed. "It doesn't have to be something obvious. Jamie was doing a lot with wine education, right? What if this has something to do with that? Maybe he got in over his head with someone in the wine world."

Abby shook her head. "That's a reach, Sara, even for you. If there's something here, it's more likely tied to his work in neurology than wine. We deal with life-and-death situations every day. One mistake, one secret... it could ruin a career."

"Or kill you" Nina interrupted.

"Yes, or kill you" Abby reiterated.

As the group mulled over Abby's words, Lori wandered toward the coffee table near the couch. Her eyes fell on the remaining bottles of champagne. Without a word, she picked one up and inspected it closely, her brow furrowing.

"What are you doing?" Traci asked.

"Look at this," Lori said, holding up the bottle. "This

isn't the usual stuff Jamie brings. He always made a big deal about getting the best vintage for our retreats. But this? It's just some plane old, generic label."

"I told you they were switched." Eve stated.

"So?" Nina said, crossing her arms.

"So," Lori continued, "Jamie would never settle for this unless he had no choice."

Traci added, "what does that label say anyway?"

"it just says 2001" Lori said curiously.

Abby joined her, taking the bottle and inspecting it herself. "You're right. He was always so particular about his wine and more specifically, his champagne. Why would he bring something so... ordinary, so generic?"

Eve's voice was ice-cold. "Maybe because he didn't pick

it. The cork had French words on it, not "2001" and like I just told you guys, its fake! The cork was swapped!"

The accusation hung in the air, thick and heavy.

"Eve, I believe you; it certainly appears that someone tampered with the champagne?" Sara said, her voice somewhat puzzled.

Eve continued, "And until we know the truth, we shouldn't rule anything out."

Abby set the shards of glass down, merely held together by the label, and looked at the group. "All right. Let's focus. If Jamie's death really wasn't an accident," She hesitated, "Then we need to be prepared for the possibility that someone here knows more than they're letting on."

Traci looked around the room, her eyes darting from face to face. "We're all in this together," she said quietly, though the words felt hollow.

"Oh, you'd like that" Eve sarcastically stated, "If that's the case, maybe I will go over here by myself because if y'all involved in this, I want no part of it."

Nina snorted, "It doesn't feel like we are in this together."

"Nina" Abby warned, but Nina held up a hand.

"No, Abby. If we're going to figure this out, we need to be honest. And right now, I don't think any of us are telling the whole truth."

Lori's discovery that Eve was correct and that someone swapped the champagne bottle raised new questions. If Jamie didn't bring it, who did? And why would they change it? As mistrust continues to grow, the group

realizes that the answers they seek may reveal more than

they're ready to face.

BOTTLE 5

SECRETS AND LIES

The group sat in strained silence after Lori's revelation about the champagne bottle. The once-cozy retreat now felt suffocating, the warmth of the crackling fire a stark contrast to the icy glares exchanged across the room.

Abby was the first to break the silence. "We need to figure out where this bottle came from."

Sara crossed her arms and leaned against the mantle. "What's the point? Even if it wasn't Jamie who brought it, that doesn't mean anything. It could have come with the house."

"Or it could mean everything," Eve countered. Her voice was sharp, her eyes flickering with suspicion. "If someone switched the cork, that proves that this was murder!"

Traci shook her head, "Listen to yourselves. We're spinning out of control. This was a tragic accident. That's it."

"Then why does it feel like we're all hiding something?" Lori asked, her voice quiet but cutting.

The words lingered, each of them wrestling with their own guilt and memories of Jamie. Nina exhaled sharply and leaned forward, her elbows resting on her knees.

"Fine," she said. "Let's get it out in the open. Jamie and

I had a fight a few days ago."

The others turned to her, startled.

"A fight about what?" Abby pressed.

Nina hesitated, her fingers fidgeting with the edge of her sweater. "He was... accusing me of dumping all the ICU patients on him, while I took all the ones that were pending discharge. He said I was always dumping and that it was affecting the team."

"Dumping?" Traci asked, frowning.

"Yeah." Nina's voice dropped. "He thought I was hiding something and trying to finish early. And maybe I was trying to leave early, but it wasn't what he thought. It is not what any of you think."

"What were you hiding?" Eve asked, narrowing her eyes.

Nina bit her lip, then looked away. "That doesn't matter. The point is, we argued. He stormed off, and I thought... I thought he'd let it go because it was stupid"

Traci shook her head. "This is what I'm talking about. Jamie was under so much pressure lately. He was constantly second-guessing everything, like he couldn't trust anyone."

Lori leaned back against the window; arms folded. "And yet, he always seemed so composed."

"Because he didn't want us to see it," Abby said softly.

"Who else is hiding something?" Eve questioned.

"Come on Eve, why are you always questioning someone?" Nina said with a smirk.

"Because I did not do this and quite possibly one of y'all did" Eve fired back.

"I resent that" Traci stated.

"You meant to say, you resemble that" Eve quickly snapped.

Traci, without response decided to give her the evilest of scowls.

Sara spoke up, her voice tinged with frustration. "But what about his messages? All those points to something bigger than just stress because of your dumping."

"Hey! I was not dumping" defensively cried Nina.

"Maybe," Abby replied. "Or maybe it was all part of the pressure he was under. We're making assumptions without any real evidence."

Lori walked back to the table and picked up a piece of the champagne bottle again. "Assumptions or not, this bottle still bothers me. If Jamie didn't bring it, then who did?"

Traci raised her hand hesitantly. "I was the first to arrive and when I walked up on the porch, that crate was sitting there."

"What?" Abby asked, her brow furrowing.

Traci nodded. "I thought it was odd, too. Jamie usually brings his own stuff, but when I asked him about it, he brushed me off. Said something about keeping it simple this time."

"That's not like him," Eve muttered.

"It's not," Lori agreed. "Jamie loved to show off his wine knowledge and collection. He wouldn't just 'keep it simple.' He always goes big."

Nina groaned and rubbed her temples. "Okay, let's say someone else brought the champagne. What are you implying? That one of us planned this? Because that's insane. Like we are responsible? Like one of us killed him?"

"Maybe not planned his death," Traci said cautiously. "But... what if someone, other than us knew Jamie was coming here? What if they were trying to push him over?"

"Push him over to what?" Sara asked, her voice trembling slightly.

"To a mistake," Traci said. "Maybe someone wanted him to lose his focus so they could attack when he was weakened and not paying attention?"

Eve's eyes narrowed. "And who would want that? You?"

Traci's face flushed. "Excuse me? I have had about

enough of you Eve"

Eve snapped. "You're always sticking your nose where it doesn't belong. Maybe you finally went too far."

"Enough!" Abby barked, silencing them. She turned to the group, her voice firm. "We're not doing this. Jamie was our friend. If there's even a chance this wasn't an accident, we owe it to him to figure it out. Together and preferably before the police get here and start asking us questions that we do not have the answers to."

The room fell silent, but the tension remained thick.

As Abby tried to regain control of the situation, Lori suggested "maybe we should search the house for more insight into what may have happened? Right now, we just have a cork and some broken glass with a weird looking, generic label."

"And a dead body" Sara added.

"Yes, a dead body" Lori confirmed.

The group stared at her in stunned silence, their minds racing with questions they weren't ready to find answers to.

BOTTLE 6

A CRYPTIC MESSAGE

The group huddled around the broken champagne bottle on the coffee table in silence, their gazes fixed on the label Lori held. It was pasted on top of another label.

"Is this... normal?" Traci asked hesitantly, breaking the silence.

"No," Sara said, her tone firm. "Champagne labels don't just have nothing written on them. This does not appear to be from a winery."

"What does it mean?" Nina asked. She glanced uneasily around the room, her arms crossed tightly over her chest.

Lori shook her head. "I don't know. But if someone switched the label or bottle, this wasn't an accident. Jamie was murdered."

Abby leaned forward, taking the cork from Lori's hand to examine it. "Jamie would've noticed if the champagne wasn't authentic. He was too meticulous for that. And what is 2001? Maybe that is a winery he loves?"

Eve scoffed. "He was meticulous about wine, for sure. Jamie did not pick this. Did one of y'all pick this?"

"Enough with the distractions theory," Traci snapped.

Abby rubbed her temples, trying to think. "Let's start again with what we know. Traci said the crate was already here when we arrived, right?"

"Yes," Traci confirmed. "But I assumed Jamie had ordered them in advance. He's done that before."

"But this time, he didn't mention it; not a peep." Lori pointed out. "And we all agree that he wasn't acting like himself."

"Acting off doesn't mean he didn't order the bottles," Eve argued.

"No, but it means we can't rule anything out, including foul play" Abby said, her voice steady. "We need to look for clues. There must be something else."

The group fanned out, searching through the kitchen and living room for anything that could explain the bottle's origin. Nina rummaged through the recycling bin, while Traci rifled through the cabinets. Abby checked the delivery box the bottles had come in, hoping for a receipt or shipping label.

"I've got something," Sara called out. She held up Jamie's phone, the screen glowing faintly in the dim light. "You checked his messages Abby, but I checked his email history. Jamie placed an online order two weeks ago, but it wasn't just for champagne. It was for red wine. An entire case of wine; 12 bottles in total."

"What?" Lori frowned. "A case of wine? then why do we only see one champagne bottle here?"

"No idea," Sara replied. "But Jamie didn't order this 2001 bottle; someone else must have. These bottles are all high-end, name brand and quite pricey, Look!"

"Wow! $300 for this bottle?" Eve said, "Oh, and here is

the La Cuvee cork one that we found on the floor in the kitchen."

Sara continued, "Yeah, certainly nothing listed here says 2001, that's for sure."

Nina pulled a crumpled piece of paper from the bottom of the delivery box. "There's something else written here," she said, squinting at the smudged handwriting. She read aloud: "'Enjoy the retreat. Hope they love their night of terror.'"

"That's creepy," Traci said, her voice barely above a whisper.

"Who signed it?" Abby asked.

"No one," Nina replied.

"That's not helpful," Eve muttered. "Why would someone send an anonymous note with a bottle of champagne?"

"To mess with him?" Traci said. "To throw him off? Maybe someone wanted him to be nervous."

"Or maybe it's connected to the other messages he got before we arrived," Lori said.

Abby froze. "Messages? What other messages?"

Lori hesitated. "I didn't want to say anything before, but I saw Jamie's phone before we left the office. He had a text from someone with a blocked number. It said, 'You know what you need to do, right?'"

"Why didn't you tell us this earlier?" Traci demanded. "Why can no one tell the truth here?"

"Hmmmm" as Eve side-eyed Traci.

"Listen! One more comment and I will be committing a

murder tonight." Traci shot back a similar glare.

"I didn't think it mattered!" Lori said. "I thought it was just work stuff; like a message from the hospital because no one knows that one of us isn't there this weekend."

"Yeah, that was so nice of Yuri to cover us but, yes, Lori, it all matters. This changes everything," Abby said firmly. "The person who sent the text must be connected to the champagne."

Sara frowned. "But why would someone go to all this trouble? Jamie didn't have enemies—at least not that I knew of."

"Maybe not enemies," Traci said softly, "but he had secrets."

As the group tried to process this new revelation, Jamie's phone buzzed on the coffee table. "A signal!"

Nina screamed. She grabbed it, her face paling as she read the screen.

"What is it?" Abby asked.

Nina turned the phone around so they could see. The message was simple but chilling:

"The job is done. I hope you are pleased."

The room fell silent, the weight of the warning settling over them like a dark cloud.

Before anyone could react, the power suddenly went out, plunging the house into darkness. A loud thud echoed from somewhere upstairs, followed by the sound of shattering glass.

"Everyone stays together," Abby whispered, her voice tight with fear. "We're not alone."

BOTTLE 7

A DISCOVERY IN THE DARK

The police were, presumably, on their way. The group of now 6 decided to explore the house in search of the etiology of the mysterious thud as well as clues that could lead to some answers.

The group could not decide which of them would venture off, so they elected to divide into pairs and have a group search the upstairs, a group search the main level, and a group search the basement.

Eve, angrily stated "Listen, I don't know if y'all involved or not, but I sure as hell do not want to pair with Traci or Sara."

"What the hell did I do?" Sara asked.

"Are you implying that I did something?" Traci chimed in.

"Well, Sara, you weren't around when Jamie collapsed and Traci, well girl, we all have questions." Eve replied.

"I will go with you" Abby interjected before Traci could even reply.

"Fine, but I am not leaving this level. In fact, to demonstrate some good faith, maybe Sara and Traci should go to the basement?" Eve suggested.

"That means, Lori and I get to check out that sound from upstairs?" Nina questioned.

"Damn right girl" Eve answered.

"This is such bullshit" Traci added.

The group fanned out, covering their assigned territory. Traci and Sara ventured down the stairs and Nina and Lori ventured up the stairs. At the top of the staircase, the window in the hall was open, wedged against a picture frame and the curtains flapping in the breeze. It appeared the window opened with such force the breeze blew a candelabra off the stand directly below and the candles appeared to be thrown all over the floor.

"Could this have been the thud?" Lori questioned

"It certainly seems possible" Nina answered as the continued into a nearby bedroom.

Downstairs, Abby and Eve had not left the living space.

Eve, more concerned with her colleagues' role in their current situation suggested "Why don't you go check out the library?"

"And leave you here? Hell no! We go together" Abby stated.

Suddenly, a loud scream was heard from what appeared to be directly above them. Abby and Eve reached the top of the staircase in record time, their hearts pounding in unison. The scream had come from the furthest bedroom, where Lori and Nina were searching. Abby flung the door open, her flashlight cutting through the shadows.

The room was eerily quiet, except for the sound of Nina's ragged breathing. Lori was crouched in the corner, pale and shaking, her hands clasped tightly over her ears. Nina stood frozen near the bed, her hand covering her mouth as she stared wide-eyed at the bedspread.

"What happened?" Abby demanded, her flashlight scanning the room.

Nina pointed toward the bed, her voice trembling. "There's... there's blood."

Abby's beam followed Nina's gesture, landing on the bedspread. A dark stain marred the crisp white fabric next to Jamie's locked duffle bag.

"What is that?" Eve asked, inching closer to the bed. Her eyes darted around the room, searching for signs of a struggle.

Lori shook her head violently, tears streaming down her face. "I didn't touch it! I swear I didn't touch anything!"

Abby stepped closer with her flashlight steady. She

examined the stain carefully, noting its peculiar placement. "Where did it come from? There's no trail leading to it."

Eve moved beside her, her sharp eyes scanning every corner of the room. "There's no blood anywhere else. No handprints. Nothing on the floor. It's just... there."

Nina's voice broke through the tense silence. "What is happening here?" Her hands trembled as she gripped the bedpost for support. "I wish the police would get here already."

The "team" bailed on any hope that EMS would arrive in time and shifted their attention to assistance from the police given their current situation.

Abby straightened, her tone firm but calm. "We're all going back downstairs. Together. We're not splitting up anymore. Where are Traci and Sara?"

As the group made their way back down the staircase, the air felt heavier, as though the house itself was pressing in on them. Every creak of the floorboards beneath their feet echoed ominously, heightening their unease.

BOTTLE 8

THE STRANGER

The air inside the cabin was thick with tension as the group reconvened in the living room. The shard of green glass sat ominously on the coffee table beside the cork.

Traci broke the silence first, her voice strained "None of this makes any sense."

"Maybe it's not supposed to," Sara replied, her voice brittle. She was seated on the armrest of the couch, her posture stiff, as though bracing herself for an invisible blow "Maybe someone's just trying to scare us."

"And where were the two of you?" Nina interjected.

Lori piled on, "Yeah, I am screaming for help and Abby and Eve came up but not the two of you."

"We were" Sara fumbled, frightened by the accusation. "We were in the cellar and never heard you."

"Never heard her?" Nina questioned.

"I feel like the EMS, who are supposedly en route heard her" Eve added.

Abby's jaw tightened, she quickly, though not quick enough, interrupted "Well, if someone is trying to scare us, it is absolutely working. That being said, we can't let fear take over. We need to stay focused."

Before anyone could respond, the sound of tires

crunching gravel broke through the tense silence.

Everyone froze, their gazes snapping to the window.

"A car," Traci whispered, her face draining of color.

"It's black. It does not appear to be the police though.

Maybe unmarked?"

"Was anyone expecting a visitor?" Nina questioned.

"Oh, yeah, sure" Sara sarcastically added.

Abby grabbed the flashlight and moved cautiously to

the door. A black sedan was parked in the front, its

sleek frame gleaming under the faint moonlight. A man

in a suit stepped out, his movements calm and

deliberate. He almost gave off *An American Psycho* kind

of vibe.

He went into the trunk, retrieved a box and headed

towards the front stairs.

The group watched from behind Abby as she cracked the door open. Her voice was steady despite the tension radiating through her frame. "Can we help you?"

The man's gaze drifted past her, settling briefly on each person standing in the living room. His expression remained unreadable. He made eye contact with each one of them but never cracked a smile or responded to Abby.

"What do you want?" anxiously exclaimed Abby.

"Jamie," he said simply. "He knows I am coming for you guys."

"What in the hell does that mean?" Traci asked.

With that statement, the group collectively backed up. Well, except Abby. The group left Abby standing in the doorway by herself.

Abby said, narrowing her eyes "Do you know what's happening here?"

The man's lips curved into a faint smile, one that didn't reach his eyes. "Enough to know that I am not supposed to say what he has planned for each and every one of you."

BOTTLE 9

PIECES OF THE PUZZLE

After setting the crate on the porch, the stranger left without saying another word. Abby creeped back inside and once again, gathered the group around the coffee table, her resolve hardening. The cabin's oppressive silence was broken only by the crackling of the fire, its flickering light casting shadows that danced across their tense faces.

"We need to figure this out. Now," she said firmly.

Traci glanced nervously at the shard of green glass lying on the table. Its jagged edge seemed to gleam maliciously in the firelight. "There has to be something we're not seeing?" She asked hesitantly.

Abby leaned forward, resting her palms on the table. "Then we start from the beginning. Jamie's death, the bottle, the man, the messages. Just everything."

Eve nodded slowly; her eyes narrowed in thought. "Let's start with the blood upstairs. There's no way it just appeared out of nowhere."

"And the cork and label," Nina added, her voice quiet but steady. "What does it mean?"

"Yes, it all comes back to the label and the cork" Abby said. "Eve is convinced that someone switched the bottle. It does not match the cork at all. Someone wanted this to happen."

Sara, who had been silent up to this point, finally spoke. "But why? And who?" Her voice wavered, betraying the fear she had been trying to suppress. "We all loved Jamie. None of us would ever..."

"We don't know that" Eve interrupted sharply, her tone edged with suspicion. "Do we? Jamie had his secrets. Maybe someone else had theirs too. Like, who knew Nina and Jamie were fighting?"

"We were not fighting" Nina exclaimed

The room fell into uneasy silence. Each member of the group shifted uncomfortably in their seats, their minds racing with unspoken doubts. Abby's gaze swept across them, lingering on each face for a moment longer than necessary. She could feel the undercurrent of mistrust thickening, threatening to tear them apart.

"Let's not start pointing fingers" Abby said firmly. "We

need to focus on the clues we have, not the ones we're imagining."

"Then where do we start?" Traci asked, wrapping her arms around herself as if trying to ward off an invisible chill.

Abby straightened, her eyes locking onto the shard of glass. "The bottle. Jamie's wine was his pride and joy. If someone tampered with it, we'll find the proof there. Do we know if there are more bottles?"

The group reluctantly divided once again, this time with clearer purpose; find bottles. Abby and Eve returned to the kitchen to inspect the wine rack, while Sara and Traci searched the dining room for anything that seemed out of place. Nina and Lori elected to reinspect the bloodstained bedroom.

In the kitchen, Abby meticulously inspected each bottle

of wine, her fingers trailing over the labels and necks. "These bottles also look odd" She paused when she reached a bottle tucked in the back of the rack. The label was slightly askew, the adhesive curling at one corner. "*I Know What You Did*" she said curiously

"Eve," Abby called, holding up the bottle. "Look at this."

Eve stepped closer, squinting at the bottle under the harsh beam of the flashlight. "What the hell does that mean? '*I Know What You Did*?'"

Abby carefully inspected the bottle only to discover a small sticker on the punt. Handwritten on that sticker was a name. Her breath caught as she gasped.

Eve's brows furrowed. "What does it say?"

Abby tilted the bottle under the light, her voice barely

above a whisper. "It says......Eve"

Upstairs, Lori and Nina worked in strained silence, their flashlights sweeping over every surface. Nina stopped abruptly; her beam fixed on the edge of the bedspread.

"Lori," she said, her voice tight. "There's something here."

Lori crossed the room, her hands trembling as she crouched beside Nina. Just visible beneath the bloodstained fabric was a small, crumpled piece of paper. Nina reached for it, unfolding it carefully.

The note was hastily written, the letters jagged and uneven, as though the writer's hand had been shaking. It read:

"After me, you will have to take care of the others."

Lori's breath hitched. "What does that mean?"

Nina shook her head, her face pale. "I don't know. But it's not good. Are we all in danger?"

In the dining room, Sara and Traci sifted through drawers and cabinets, their nerves fraying with each passing minute. Traci opened a drawer filled with placemats and napkins, her fingers brushing against something hard and metallic. She pulled it out slowly, her heart pounding.

"Sara," she whispered, holding up the object. It was a corkscrew, its handle stained with something dark and dried.

Sara's face went pale as she stared at it. "Is that... blood?"

Traci quietly nodded, placing the corkscrew on the table between them. The two women exchanged a look, the implications settling heavily over them.

The group reconvened in the living room, their findings laid out on the coffee table: the scratched bottle, the bloodstained corkscrew, and the ominous note from upstairs. Abby looked at each item in turn, her mind racing to piece together the puzzle.

"*I Know What You Did* Eve," she said, pointing to the bottle. "Someone wanted us to find this."

"Come on! I am not involved, and the bottle does not say that – well at least not the way you just said it" Eve asked. "And what the hell is that supposed to mean?"

"You tell us Eve" Nina said with a scowl.

"Shut up heffa!" Eve snapped back

Lori explained the letter she found, "It seems whoever did this is not remotely finished."

Abby's jaw tightened. "Calm down everyone. Maybe

someone here is next and not necessarily involved in the

killing. But then that would mean that whoever is

behind this isn't finished yet."

"Killing? Next? Not finished?" questioned Eve

BOTTLE 10

REVELATIONS

The time stretched on as the group combed through the cabin, searching for anything that could provide clarity. The oppressive atmosphere of the cabin grew heavier with every passing minute. Shadows seemed to deepen, and the howling wind outside carried an almost taunting rhythm. Abby sat alone in the living room, turning the shard of green glass over in her hands, its edges catching the dim glow of the firelight. Her thoughts swirled chaotically, replaying every detail of the past day.

Abby looked at the other bottles found in the kitchen. One bottle stated '*Psycho.*' She turned the bottle upside-down and very similar to the first bottle which pointed at Eve, she found the word...... "Sara?" She questioned out loud. "Uh, Sara, can you come in here?"

Sara darted around the corner, what's up?"

"This label says you are a *psycho*" Abby explained.

"A *psycho?* Me?" questioned Sara. "Jamie and I have had our disagreements, but to call me a psycho is a bit dramatic. How about the other bottle? Does it call someone else psycho?"

"Well, this label says *Cat People*" Abby stated.

"Gee, let me guess that one. Bet it says Abby" Sara said with an attitude.

Abby turned the bottle upside-down and sure enough, almost disappointingly, Abby said "yes, yes it does say me."

"But you are a cat person, Abby. Does that really mean he thought I was a *psycho?*" Sara said quite upset.

The faint sound of footsteps broke her concentration. She looked up sharply, her heart pounding. Lori stood in the doorway, her expression hesitant and almost afraid.

"Hey Abby, can I talk to you?" Lori asked softly.

Abby nodded, motioning for her to sit. "What's on your mind?" as she left Sara and went to speak with Lori.

Lori hesitated, her hands twisting in her lap. "I've been thinking a lot about what happened."

Abby leaned forward, studying Lori's face intently. "We

all have, what are you talking about?"

Lori's voice dropped to a whisper, as though afraid someone might overhear. "What if...I mean; I know what Jamie said to us 'It wasn't an accident' but with all these clues, I am really concerned that Jamie knew what was going to happen and we are next. What if he was right and it wasn't an accident?"

Abby's brow furrowed. "You think someone did this on purpose, Jamie knew, and they may be after us?"

Lori nodded slowly, her gaze darting to the floor. "I don't know who would do this, but... the bottles, the messages, the blood. It's all too much to be a coincidence."

"I agree Lori, I mean, this bottle does seem to tell us that Eve is also hiding something. Then, we find out Nina and Traci had their run-ins with Jamie as well."

"Exactly! In the last 45 minutes, we have learned so much about one another and the skeletons we may have." Lori reaffirmed Abby's thinking.

Abby's grip tightened on the shard of glass. "Then we need to figure out who did this and why."

Lori hesitated, biting her lip. "But what if... what if it's one of us?"

Abby's stomach twisted. The possibility had crossed her mind (all their minds), but hearing Lori voice it made it feel disturbingly real. "I don't want to believe that" she said carefully. "But we can't rule anything out."

"But I mean the bottle, what if Eve was hiding something that Jamie knew about, and she decided to take him out for it?" Lori explained

The crackling fire filled the silence between them, a

stark contrast to the tension in the room. Abby reached out, placing a hand on Lori's arm. "Eve is good people, she would never, and I am not sure it means anything because this bottle basically states I like cats."

"Which is true!" Lori stated. "So, if that is true, then the others must be."

"So, Sara is a psycho?" Abby questioned.

Lori met Abby's gaze, her eyes glistening with unshed tears. "I swear, I don't know anything. I just... I feel like we are missing something. Like there's something Jamie wanted us to find."

Abby nodded, her mind racing. "We'll find it," she said firmly. "We have to."

Meanwhile, Traci and Sara were back in the dining room, their search continuing with mounting frustration. Sara sifted through a pile of papers they'd found in a drawer, her hands trembling slightly. "This is useless," she muttered. "Receipts, takeout menus... nothing that explains any of this."

Traci, who had been inspecting the underside of the dining table, straightened abruptly. "Wait," she said, her voice sharp. "What if we're not looking for something obvious? We already searched his phone, so, what if more clues are in his suitcase?"

Sara frowned. "You mean the duffel he brought?"

"It is upstairs next to the blood" Lori added.

The group hesitantly but collectively rushed upstairs to the blood-stained room. The bag lay on the bed where it was originally placed by Jamie less than an hour ago. Unfortunately, the team realized there was a combination lock on it.

Sara's breath caught. "Do you think? Why would he have a lock on it?"

"He travelled a lot" Nina added. "He was always heading to some place so maybe he had a lock for TSA or maybe just to keep his kids out."

"Or to keep secrets hidden" Eve said mysteriously.

Sara leaned in closer, inspecting it. "We'll need a code. It is a 3-digit lock.

Traci's mind raced. "Jamie loved puzzles. He wouldn't make it obvious."

Sara pulled his phone from her pocket that for some reason she was still carrying around.

"Hey! Why do you still have that?" Nina called out.

Anxious and surprised, Sara "uhhh, in case more

messages came in." Sara then scrolled and scrolled but found nothing. She suddenly and without a question screamed "911. Could that be it? The number he always wrote on the whiteboard. 'In Case of Emergency don't call us, call 911!'"

Traci quickly rolled the numbers into the lock. The lock opened, and sitting on top of all his clothes was a single envelope, sealed and marked with Jamie's handwriting: "To my friends."

Sara and Traci exchanged a look, their hearts pounding. Traci reached for the envelope, her hands shaking as she opened it. Inside was a single sheet of paper, covered in Jamie's familiar scrawl.

"To all of my friends on this ominous night – A night of horror is upon you."

BOTTLE 11

THE FINAL CLUE

The group gathered in the living room once more, the note from the duffle bag placed carefully on the coffee table. The fire had burned down to embers, casting flickering shadows that danced across their faces. Abby read the note aloud, her voice steady but tense.

"Seven friends gathered together for a night of horror"

Abby paused, her eyes scanning the page. "Everything

you need to know is in the bottles. Trust the wine."

"Trust the wine?" Eve repeated, her tone incredulous. "What the hell does that mean? Trust that Sara is a *psycho?*"

"Hey!!" Sara shouted back. "Trust that he knows what you did!"

"And what do you think I did?" Eve was immediately interrupted.

"Shut it ladies!" Abby set the note down, her mind racing. "Trust the wine. If there is a clue, this must be it, right?"

Traci leaned forward; her gaze fixed on the scratched bottles they'd found earlier. "*I know what you did* Eve. Sara is a *psycho,* and Abby is a cat person."

Eve hesitated. "None of this makes sense. Like, what in

the hell does Abby liking cats have to do with wine or the murder?"

Abby nodded. "Maybe we should see what was also delivered?"

"The crate!" Traci said excitedly.

The group bundled up against the cold, stepping outside into the biting night air. The box on the front porch of the lake house, the beam of their flashlights cutting through the darkness. Every creak of the wood underfoot sent shivers down their spines.

"This is insane," Sara muttered, pulling her jacket tighter around herself. "What are we even looking for?"

"We'll know when we find it," Abby replied, though she wasn't entirely sure she believed it.

After what felt like forever, the group re-entered the

house. They placed the large wooden crate on the floor of the foyer. Abby stepped forward cautiously, pulling away the label only to reveal a carved insignia of a wine bottle.

"This is it," she said, her voice barely above a whisper.

She pried the crate open, revealing a collection of bottles, each marked with a single word.

BOTTLE 12

THE TRUTH REVEALED

Back at the cabin, the group gathered around the table, the bottles of wine laid out before them. Each label bore a different label and word.

"What is this?" Lori asked, her voice trembling. Her gaze darted from one bottle to the next, her confusion mirroring the growing unease in the room.

Abby picked up the first bottle that said "Jamie",

inspecting the label and the word etched on its label.

"These bottles; each one of them; they're tied to us," she murmured. "But this one; the one that says 'Jamie;' that bottle is super light." She twisted the cap off the bottle; her movements deliberate and poured its contents into a glass. What emerged was not wine, but a paper tightly rolled up. She unfolded it, her eyes narrowing as she read the words to herself.

"Jamie dying was just an accident." She exclaimed.

The room fell silent. Each person exchanged stunned glances, the weight of the revelation pressing down on them. Abby's grip tightened on the slip of paper as she opened another bottle, revealing a similar note: "Enjoy the wine and a weekend of thriller movies."

"How is this an accident?" Traci questioned. Her voice barely audible. "None of what we discovered sounds like an accident. None of it at all."

Abby removed the bottles one by one and at the bottom of the crate were a bunch of old VHS tapes. Each tape had the same word as a correlating bottle.

One by one, they looked at the bottles, each containing a single word and that word correlated with a VHS tape.

Carrie

Scream

Exorcist

Poltergeist

Nosferatu

Hostel

Saw

Shining

Abby stood; the last note clutched in her hand. Her voice was steady but heavy with emotion. "He didn't mean for any of this to happen. The cork... the switched labels it was an elaborate gift. Jamie was trying to give us a bottle of wine and a VHS tape, look!" she said excitedly "our names on the bottle and VHS tapes. Eve got *I Know What You Did Last Summer*. Look! Your name is on a list and correlates with a movie.

"I told you I didn't do anything" Eve exclaimed.

Abby continued "Sara got *Psycho*. I got *Cat People*. Lori got the *Exorcist*. Traci got *Poltergeist*. Nina got *Scream*. Jamie had the labels from the VHS tapes turned into wine labels for the bottle and had each of our names etched on the punt of the bottle.

"So, that's why the cork did not match the label of

2001." Eve shouted out, her excitement breaking through.

"So that's why the cork did not have any glass attached to it." Sara explained.

"What do you mean?" Eve questioned.

"Well, if Traci dropped a bottle with the cork in it, then the glass shattering would have been the thing that released the pressure in the bottle and therefore the cork would have had the glass neck still wrapped around it. But, because the cork already went flying, by the time Traci picked up the bottle"

"On my way in" Traci interrupted.

"Yes, on her way in" Sara added. "By the time Traci picked up the bottle, the cork had already released from the bottle therefore having no glass around it. Then, when Traci dropped the bottle, it shattered but the cork was already gone."

"Why didn't he just tell us about the bottles?" Nina asked.

Abby's gaze softened. "Because he wanted to give us a gift and maybe watch a few films. Especially scary films here a desolate lake house. Jamie loved puzzles. He probably thought this would be fun."

Lori's voice trembled. "But the blood... the corkscrew... the notes in the bottles. How do you explain that?"

Abby turned toward the fire, her expression contemplative. " The blood..." She hesitated, piecing it together. "That must've been from Jamie himself from something unrelated. A red herring per se. But that was Jamie's corkscrew in the kitchen, wasn't it?"

"The waiter's key" Traci quickly corrected her.

"Yes, the waiter's key. Maybe when he brought it downstairs from his bag, he poked himself which dropped blood on the floor and was left on the corkscrew, because maybe he didn't even know he got stuck?" Abby explained. "Check his finger."

"Yep, on his right index finger, there is dried blood" Nina reported.

Abby continued, "I bet the force of the cork hitting his temple likely caused an injury that bled internally and there was nothing we could have done."

"Jamie always said those corks can go flying at 65miles per hour in some instances." Traci added.

Abby continued "He went to open the bottle, we all walked away, he sat the bottle down"

"And BAM!" Lori interjected.

"Yes, and bam" Abby said with less enthusiasm. "The cork dislodged, hitting the side of his head."

"So, it really was just an accident?" Nina said, her voice breaking the silence. "He tried to do something nice, and it killed him."

"Stop it" Sara stated.

Abby nodded, her heart aching. "Jamie loved to play games. And, unfortunately, this one went totally wrong..." She trailed off, staring at the notes spread across the table. "It was just a terrible accident."

The group sat in stunned silence; the nightmare they'd been living unraveling before them. The tension and suspicion that had built up over the past hour began to dissolve, replaced by a profound sadness.

"Why didn't we see it sooner?" Sara asked, her voice cracking. "We spent all this time thinking the worst. About him. About each other."

Abby placed a comforting hand on Sara's shoulder. "Because fear does that to people. It clouds judgment. Jamie picked horror movies here, in the middle of nowhere. And unfortunately, it really did become a horror movie for all of us."

Outside, the moonlight broke through the trees, casting the cabin in a warm, white glow. The fire had burned down to embers, its warmth a faint reminder of the long night they had endured. One by one, the group began to pick up the pieces, their grief mingling with a newfound sense of clarity.

Abby stood by the window, watching as the Police and EMS arrived. She clutched the last words tightly in her soul, Jamie's final message echoing in her mind: 'It wasn't an accident.' But she now questioned whether he may have said, 'It was an accident.' Though the truth had been uncovered, its weight would stay with them forever, a reminder of the fragility of life and the importance of forgiveness.

EPILOGUE

Months later, the group gathered again, this time in a bustling beer and wine shop which was hours away from the cabin and within a mile of their southern-most office. The atmosphere was lighter, yet a shadow lingered in their shared glances and quiet moments. They hadn't planned to meet anytime soon, but Jamie's memory pulled them back together.

Abby held her Chardonnay, her mind drifting to the bottles, the messages, and the overwhelming grief that had bound them all together that night. Despite their efforts to move on, something still nagged at her—a thread left untied.

"It's strange," Traci said, breaking the silence. "I thought finding out the truth would bring closure. But I still feel like we're missing something."

"You're not alone," Lori admitted. "I can't stop thinking about those messages we read. Jamie knew something we didn't. The blood, the corkscrew? None of it makes sense to me."

Abby exhaled deeply, setting her spoon down. "I've been thinking about that too. Jamie was very meticulous. Every detail mattered to him. If he swapped the labels, and we think he had a reason. What if there's more to this than we realized?"

Eve frowned. "Abby, we went over everything. The

messages, the bottles, the blood. We pieced it together. It was an accident. He even said it himself."

"Maybe" Abby conceded. "But doesn't it bother you that I am not entirely sure he didn't say that it wasn't an accident? Lori said herself that she heard Jamie state that it wasn't an accident."

"I swear that is what I heard" Lori reiterated.

The table fell silent. Each of them wrestled with the question, their unease resurfacing.

"You think someone else was involved?" Sara asked cautiously. "That maybe... Jamie knew?"

Abby shook her head. "I don't know. But I keep wondering if we were supposed to find more."

As they sat in contemplative silence, a male server, dressed in a suit, greased up hair, approached the team, placing a bottle of wine on the table. The label was plain, but a familiar inscription caught Abby's eye: "Trust the wine"

Her heart stopped. She exchanged a wide-eyed look with the others before picking up the bottle. A small card was attached, bearing a single line of text: "The truth will set you free."

The group froze, the weight of the message sinking in. Abby's grip tightened on the bottle as a cold realization settled over her. They hadn't reached the end of the story—only the beginning of another chapter.

ABOUT THE AUTHOR

Dr. Jesse V. McClain IV, DNP, APRN, CCRN, MSCN, SCRN, FWS is a distinguished healthcare professional, researcher, and author with a passion for both neurology and wine. As an Advanced Practice Registered Nurse specializing in neurology and stroke care, Dr. McClain has contributed extensively to medical research, with publications in prestigious journals and involvement in numerous clinical studies.

Beyond the medical field, Dr. McClain is an accomplished writer and wine expert. He is the author of *The Wine Doctor: Wine for Beginners from a Doctor of Nursing Practice and French Wine Scholar* and *The French Wine Workbook*. Certified by The Wine & Spirits Education Trust and a French Wine Scholar, he combines his scientific expertise with a deep appreciation for viticulture.

In addition to his medical and literary achievements, Dr. McClain is a former professional marathoner and an internationally ranked pinball competitor. His diverse interests and dedication to lifelong learning continue to inspire both his patients and readers alike.

CHECK OUT OUR OTHER WORKS

The Wine Doctor: Wine for beginners from a Doctor of
Nursing Practice and French Wine Scholar
ISBN 979-8-9870045-1-7

The French Wine Workbook
ISBN 979-8-9870045-5-5

Be sure to follow us on Twitter - @vannysvineyards

Be sure to follow us on TikTok - @thewinedrjesse

Check out our website – www.vannysvineyards.com

THANK YOU

www.ingramcontent.com/pod-product-compliance
Lightning Source LLC
Chambersburg PA
CBHW030543130626
46552CB00006B/2391